DAN YACCARINO'S

Mother goose

Illustrated by Dan Yaccarino to honor 60 years of Little Golden Books

A GOLDEN BOOK · NEW YORK

Copyright © 2003 by Random House, Inc. All rights reserved under International and Pan-American Copyright Conventions. Published in the United States by Golden Books, an imprint of Random House Children's Books, a division of Random House, Inc., New York, and simultaneously in Canada by Random House of Canada Limited, Toronto. Golden Books, A Golden Book, A Little Golden Book, the G colophon, and the distinctive gold spine are registered trademarks of Random House, Inc. A Little Golden Book is a trademark of Random House, Inc. Library of Congress Control Number: 2002113526
ISBN: 0-375-82571-1
www.goldenbooks.com
PRINTED IN CHINA   First Random House Edition 2003
10 9 8 7 6 5 4 3 2 1

Old Mother Goose,
When she wanted to wander,
Would ride through the air
On a very fine gander.

Hickety, pickety, my fine hen,
She lays eggs for gentlemen;
Gentlemen come every day
To see what my fine hen doth lay.
Sometimes nine and
 sometimes ten,
Hickety, pickety, my fine hen.

To market, to market, to buy a fat pig,
Home again, home again, jiggety-jig;
To market, to market, to buy a fat hog,
Home again, home again, jiggety-jog.

Simple Simon met a pieman
Going to the fair;
Said Simple Simon to the pieman,
"Let me taste your ware."

Said the pieman to Simple Simon,
"Show me first your penny."
Said Simple Simon to the pieman,
"Indeed, I have not any."

Three wise men of Gotham
Went to sea in a bowl.
And if the bowl had been stronger,
My song had been longer.

Little Miss Muffet
Sat on a tuffet,
Eating her curds and whey.
Along came a spider,
Who sat down beside her,
And frightened Miss Muffet away.

Peter, Peter, pumpkin eater,
Had a wife and couldn't keep her;

He put her in a pumpkin shell,
And there he kept her very well.

Doctor Foster went to Glo'ster,
In a shower of rain;
He stepped in a puddle, up to his middle,
And never went there again.

Handy Pandy, Jack-a-dandy
Loves plum cake and sugar candy.
He bought some at a grocer's shop,
And out he came, hop, hop, hop!

Jack Sprat could eat no fat,
His wife could eat no lean.
And so between them both, you see,
They licked the platter clean.

Little Bo-Peep has lost her sheep,
And can't tell where to find them.
Leave them alone, and they'll come home,
Wagging their tails behind them.

Peter Piper picked a peck of pickled peppers;
A peck of pickled peppers Peter Piper picked.
If Peter Piper picked a peck of pickled peppers,
Where's the peck of pickled peppers Peter Piper picked?

Tom, Tom, the piper's son,
Learned to play when he was young.
But the only tune that he could play
Was "Over the Hills and Far Away!"

"Bow, wow, wow!"
"Whose dog art thou?"
"Little Tom Tinker's dog,
Bow, wow, wow!"

Mary had a little lamb, with fleece as white as snow;
And everywhere that Mary went the lamb was sure
  to go.
It followed her to school one day—that was against
  the rule.
It made the children laugh and play to see a lamb
  at school.

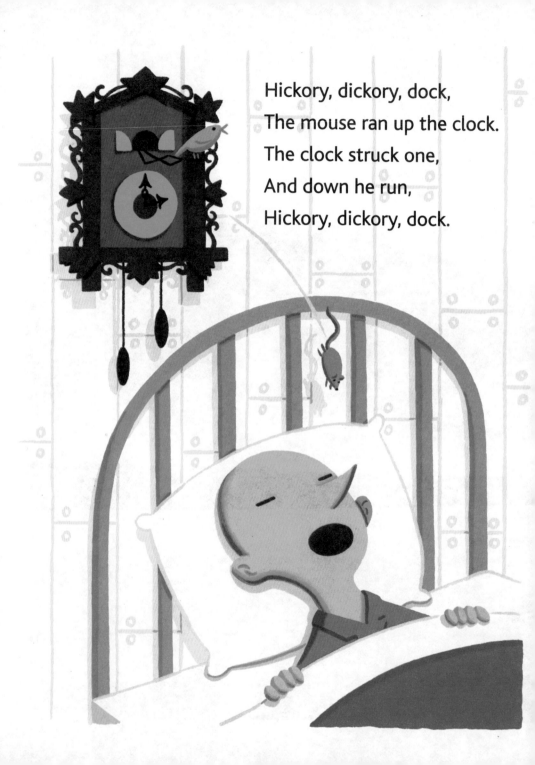

Hickory, dickory, dock,
The mouse ran up the clock.
The clock struck one,
And down he run,
Hickory, dickory, dock.

Wee Willie Winkie runs through the town,
Upstairs and downstairs, in his nightgown,
Tapping at the window, crying at the lock,
"Are the babes in their beds? For it's now eight o'clock."

The Man in the Moon looked out of the moon
And this is what he said,
"'Tis time for all children on earth
To think about getting to bed!"